Alain Serge Dzotap is a Cameroonian children's author and poet. Born in Bafoussam, he started to write poetry after devouring book after book from the city library. Today he promotes literacy across Cameroon through workshops, school visits, and his publishing house Les Bruits de l'encre. Alain's books have received the Saint-Exupéry Valeurs Jeunesse Prize and have been included in the International Youth Library's White Ravens catalog. In 2016, Alain was recognized with Cameroon's medal of knight. *The Gift* is his first book published in English.

Delphine Renon is a French illustrator, ceramicist, and graphic designer. Her books include *The Quiet Crocodile* (Princeton Architectural) and *Emmett and Caleb* (Book Island), which was nominated for the 2020 Kate Greenaway Medal. Visit Delphine's website at delphinerenon.blogspot.fr or follow her on Instagram @delphinerenon.

First published in the United States in 2022 by Eerdmans Books for Young Readers, an imprint of Wm. B. Eerdmans Publishing Co., Grand Rapids, Michigan
www.eerdmans.com/youngreaders • Text © 2020 Alain Serge Dzotap • Illustrations © 2020 Delphine Renon • Originally published in France as *Le Cadeau*, © 2020 Les éditions des éléphants
English-language translation © Eerdmans Books for Young Readers 2022 • This edition was published by arrangement with The Picture Book Agency, France
All rights reserved • Manufactured in China • 30 29 28 27 26 25 24 23 22   1 2 3 4 5 6 7 8 9 • ISBN 978-0-8028-5583-1
A catalog record of this book is available from the Library of Congress • Illustrations created with colored pencil and ink

MIX
Paper from
responsible sources
www.fsc.org
FSC® C104723

The Gift

Alain Serge Dzotap • Delphine Renon

EERDMANS BOOKS FOR YOUNG READERS

GRAND RAPIDS, MICHIGAN

Leo received many beautiful presents for his birthday.

But the one he likes best of all is his father's gift: a pen.

"There are all sorts of beautiful things inside your pen," Papa tells him.

"When I come back from the market later, I'll show them to you."

Mama is busy, and Leo doesn't want to wait.
He tries to get the beautiful things out of his pen—
all on his own. But nothing comes out.

So Leo goes to find his big sister.
"Papa says there are beautiful things inside my pen.
Can you help me get them out?"

His sister is surprised.
She takes the pen and shakes it.
A few drops of ink slip out.

"You're not doing it right," Leo says,
and he leaves.

Leo goes to find Coco-Tembo, the hen, and asks for her help getting the beautiful things out of his pen. Coco-Tembo says, "Your pen is barely bigger than an egg—how can there be beautiful things inside it?"

So Leo leaves.

Leo goes to find Super-Zombo, the giraffe, and asks for her help getting the beautiful things out of his pen.

"This isn't a pen—it's a flute!"
says Super-Zombo immediately.
She blows and blows,
but no music comes out.

"You're not doing it right," says Leo,
and he leaves.

Leo returns home.
He can't wait any longer.
He asks his mother:
"Mama, can you please show me the
beautiful things that are inside my pen?"

"Come with me," Mama says.

Mama sets a sheet of paper in front of Leo.

Holding his paw in hers, she helps him move the pen slowly across the page.

Leo asks: "What's that? What's that?"

"We just wrote *Leo*," Mama answers.

Leo is surprised. "My name is in the pen?"

"Yes," answers his mother. "Your name and all the words in the world."

Leo asks, "Is there *cake* in my pen?"

"Yes," his mother answers, and they write the word *cake*.

"And *train*?"

"*Train*, too," she answers.

"Even *plane*?"

"Even *plane*."

Leo and Mama write as many words as they can think of.

Leo continues on his own.
He draws mountains, the ocean, the sun.
Soon the whole world is coming out of his pen!

When Papa returns, he comes up quietly behind Leo and says, "What beautiful things you've found in your pen, Leo! Well done, my darling—you're a natural!"